Where Will You Sleep

by
Stephanie Shea

AuthorHouse™
1663 Liberty Drive, Suite 200
Bloomington, IN 47403
www.authorhouse.com
Phone: 1-800-839-8640

AuthorHouse™ UK Ltd.
500 Avebury Boulevard
Central Milton Keynes, MK9 2BE
www.authorhouse.co.uk
Phone: 08001974150

First published by AuthorHouse 8/9/2006

ISBN: 1-4259-3087-5 (sc)

Library of Congress Control Number: 2006903724

Printed in the United States of America
Bloomington, Indiana

This book is printed on acid-free paper.

Bloomington, IN

Milton Keynes, UK

Dedication

To my son, Hunter, I dedicate this book. You are my inspiration. You bring joy to my life. Believe in yourself and you can accomplish anything you put your mind too. I love you!

To you Dad – I want to thank you for being a part of this book. The pictures are great! Thank you for believing in me and always supporting me. Thank you!!

Mom, I also want to thank you for believing in me. You always encourage me to do what I want. Thank you!!

Thank you God for blessing me.

The moon is shining.
The stars are bright.
Where will you be sleeping tonight?

HOME
SWEET
HOME

In a cave,

Or on a rock,

Inside a barn,

Or nestled in a sock?

Down a burrow,

Up a tree,

On a lily pad,

Or under the sea?

Oh no, oh no, oh no, not me.
These are not places for me, you see.

In my bed I'll be tucked in tight,
My mommy will kiss me and say "good night."

About the Author

After eight years of teaching elementary school, Stephanie Shea plunged into the world of children's literature. She decided to turn her dream of writing into a reality after seeing her four year old son's love for books. As a mother, she realized how important her actions would play as an example to her son and his decisions in life.